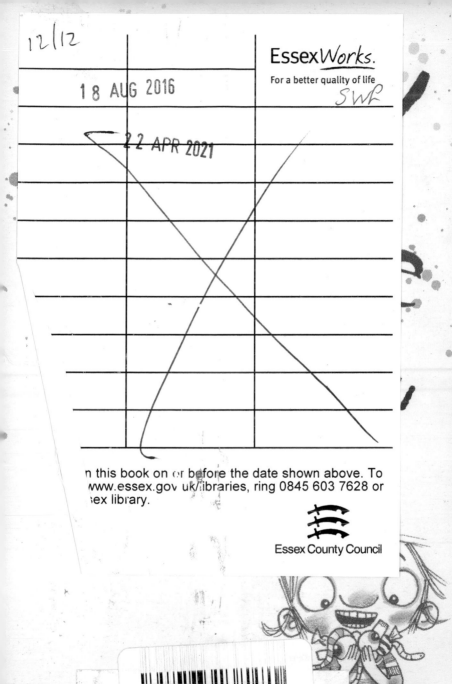

12/12

For Helen ~ D R

For Lorin, with best wishes ~ A M

STRIPES PUBLISHING
An imprint of Little Tiger Press
1 The Coda Centre, 189 Munster Road,
London SW6 6AW

A paperback original
First published in Great Britain in 2012

Characters created by David Roberts
Text copyright © Alan MacDonald, 2012
Illustrations copyright © David Roberts, 2012

ISBN: 978-1-84715-244-2

Printed and bound in the UK.

10 9 8 7 6 5 4 3 2 1

Dirty Bertie

SCREAM!

DAVID ROBERTS WRITTEN BY ALAN MACDONALD

stripes

Collect all the Dirty Bertie books!

Contents

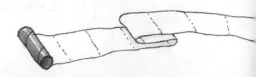

CHAPTER 1

Bertie sprang out from behind the door with a blood-curdling roar.

"RAAAARGH!"

"ARGHH!" screamed Mum, spilling her coffee everywhere. "Bertie! Don't do that, you scared the life out of me!"

"It's my monster mask," said Bertie. "It's *meant* to scare you."

Bertie pulled off the mask. It was brilliant — bright green with pointed ears, yellow fangs and three eyes. Wait till his friends saw it.

"Where did you get it?" asked Mum.

"From the shop. It's for Halloween," said Bertie. "I'm going trick-or-treating."

"Oh no, you're not," said Mum.

Bertie gaped. "Why not?"

"Because last year we got complaints," said Mum. "You almost gave Mrs Nicely a heart attack."

"That wasn't my fault," said Bertie. How was he to know Mrs Nicely was scared of bats? Even plastic ones. Some people had no sense of humour!

"Anyway, Darren and Eugene are going," said Bertie. "I promised them."

"I don't care what you promised,"

replied Mum. "Besides, it's Suzy's concert tonight and we are going."

"What — I am?" said Bertie.

"No, you're staying at home. Gran is coming to babysit," said Mum. "You can watch a nice film together."

Bertie groaned. Watching a film with Gran — on Halloween night? Some treat! Everyone else would be dressing up to go trick-or-treating. And Halloween was the best night of the year for sweets. Toffees, liquorice, lollipops, gummy bears — every house handed out sweets on Halloween. If he didn't go, he would miss it all!

"What about Darren and Eugene?" he said. "They can't go without me!"

"Well, if it matters so much, why don't you invite them here? You could have a Halloween party. Dress up and play some games," said Mum.

Bertie wasn't convinced. "But what about the sweets?" he said. "We always get sweets on Halloween!"

"Fine," sighed Mum. "I'll leave out some squash and biscuits."

Bertie stomped out of the room clutching his monster mask. A glass of squash and a few measly biscuits? This was going to be the worst Halloween night ever!

CHAPTER 2

At six o'clock Bertie slouched in the hall as his parents got ready to go out.

"Right," said Mum. "I've left some jelly eyeballs for any trick-or-treaters. I'm leaving you in charge, Bertie."

"And that doesn't mean you can eat them," warned Dad.

"Not even one?" said Bertie.

Dirty Bertie

"No! They're for people who come to the door," said Mum. "Gran will be keeping an eye on you, won't you, Gran?"

"Mmm?" said Gran, who was glued to *Animal Olympics* on the TV. "Yes, off you go. We'll be fine, won't we, Bertie?"

The front door slammed. Bertie drooped into the kitchen and stared at the jelly eyeballs in the bowl. It was torture leaving sweets out that he wasn't allowed to eat. He bet he was the only one in his class whose parents starved them of sweets on Halloween. It would serve them right if he died of hunger!

DING DONG!

Bertie hurried to the door. It was his friends. Eugene was dressed as a ghost, while Darren had come as Splat-man.

"TRICK OR TREAT?" they yelled.

Bertie's shoulders drooped. "I can't come out."

"WHAT? Why not?" cried Darren.

Bertie shrugged. "Mum won't let me."

"But you've got to, we're going trick-or-treating!" said Eugene, from under his sheet.

"I know!" sighed Bertie. "It's not my fault. Mum says we can stay here. Gran's babysitting."

13

Darren and Eugene looked at each other. It was hardly what they had in mind.

"Got any sweets?" asked Darren.

"Jelly eyeballs," nodded Bertie. "But I'm not allowed to touch them. They're for people who come to the door."

Darren shrugged. "We've come to the door."

"That's true," agreed Bertie. "And if you think about it, I've come to the door to let you in."

"Exactly," said Darren.

Ten minutes later the sweets had all gone. They sat round the kitchen table, staring at the pumpkin lantern Bertie had made. Darren let out a long sigh.

"This is boring! We should go trick-or-treating."

Bertie rolled his eyes. "How many times? I'm not allowed."

"We are, though," said Darren.

Bertie glared.

"We could call at Know-All Nick's house and haunt him," said Eugene.

Bertie suddenly sat up. He'd just had a brilliant idea. This way they could get their hands on tons of sweets without even leaving the house.

"I've got it!" he cried. "A haunted house!"

"Eh?" said Eugene. "Where?"

"Here!" said Bertie. "We'll make one like the one at the fair."

"You mean with spooky music and evil laughter," said Darren. "MUH HA HA HA!"

"Yes! And cobwebs and cupboards with skeletons in!" said Bertie.

Eugene looked doubtful. "But who's going to see it?" he asked.

"Anyone who comes trick-or-treating!" cried Bertie. "And here's the best bit – they have to pay us in sweets to come in."

He could see it now – a haunted house with creaking stairs and rattling doors. Witches in the attic, ghosts in the bedrooms and zombies in the toilet.

It would be scarier than Miss Boot on a Monday morning. Once word got round, people would be queuing down the road to get in. They'd be rolling in sweets.

"Hang on, though," said Darren. "What about the ghosts?"

"I can be a ghost," cried Eugene, ducking under his sheet. "WOOOO! WOOOOOO!"

Bertie sighed. Eugene's ghost impression wouldn't frighten a two-year-old. No, they would have to think of something really spooky, something to totally scare the pants off people.

"What if one of us was dressed as a vampire?" suggested Darren.

"Or a skeleton," said Eugene.

"I know!" said Bertie. "What about … a MUMMY?"

Brilliant! They'd
been doing the
Egyptians at
school and
mummies
were the
creepiest things alive
(or dead, for that matter).
Imagine it, thought
Bertie – a haunted
tomb filled with weird
paintings and statues ... then a coffin lid
slides back and something terrible rises
out of the dark. An ancient mummy, a
million years old...

"It could work," said Darren. "But
who's going to be the mummy?"

"Not me," said Eugene quickly. "I'm not
lying in a coffin. My mum wouldn't like it."

"Well, I can't," said Bertie. "I've got to answer the door. It has to be Darren."

"Me?" said Darren. "I'd rather be Splat-man."

Upstairs in Bertie's bedroom, they stood back to admire their work. Darren was wrapped from head to toe in toilet paper. Only his mouth was visible, and a tuft of hair sticking up like a carrot top. Bertie thought he looked dead creepy – he certainly wouldn't want to meet him in a deep dark tomb.

"Fantastic!" he said. "Say something."

"URRRGHHHHHH!" moaned Darren, who didn't know a lot of Egyptian.

"Not bad. Try walking around," said Eugene.

Dirty Bertie

Darren raised his arms and shuffled forward mummy-style, trailing bits of tissue.

"URRGH … URGHHHH … OWWW!" he cried, walking into the bed. It was hard to see where you were going, wrapped in toilet paper.

"It's okay," said Bertie, steering him in the right direction. "You don't need to see. Just lie still and act dead."

CHAPTER 3

DING DONG! Their first customers had arrived.

Bertie thumped downstairs and skidded into the hall.

"Is that the door?" asked Gran, peering out of the lounge.

"It's okay, I'll get it," said Bertie. "It's probably just people trick-or-treating."

Dirty Bertie

At the door was Know-All Nick, dressed as Frankenstein's monster. He had a green face, an ugly scar and two plastic bolts in his neck. Bertie thought it was a big improvement. He eyed the bulging bag of sweets in Nick's hand.

"Oh, it's you," sneered Nick. "Trick or treat?"

"Wait there," said Bertie.

He disappeared and came back with a broken biscuit.

"What's this? Where's my sweets?"
bleated Nick.

"Umm … someone ate them," said
Bertie.

Nick folded his arms. "You have to give
me a treat or I'm not going."

"Okay," said Bertie. "Want to see
something scary?"

"What, your face?" sniggered Nick.

"No, actually," said Bertie. He looked
around and lowered his voice. "A
haunted house."

"Oh, HA HA!" said Nick. "As if."

Bertie shrugged. "Okay, don't believe
me," he said, starting to close the door.
"You had your chance."

"WAIT!" cried Nick. "Where?"

"You're looking at it," said Bertie.
"The most haunted house in the world.

You should be here at night. I've seen things that'd give you nightmares."

"What?" gasped Nick.

"Ghosts," hissed Bertie.

Nick gulped. He'd never seen a ghost.

"I don't believe you," he said. "Prove it."

"Step this way," said Bertie. "Only ten sweets for the round tour of the Horrible Haunted House."

"TEN SWEETS?" squawked Nick.

"Eight for children," said Bertie.

Nick scowled. This was one of Bertie's tricks to make a fool of him. There was no way he lived in a haunted house. On the other hand, what if he wasn't making it up? After all, it was Halloween, the night that ghouls and ghosts came out.

"Okay, you're on," he said, holding out his bag of sweets. "But I'm counting them."

Bertie helped himself to three big fat gobstoppers, a lollipop and some lemon sherbets. Then he led the way upstairs where Eugene was waiting on the landing with a pumpkin lantern. The lights were off and the door to Bertie's bedroom was closed.

"What's in there?" asked Nick nervously.

"You'll soon find out," said Bertie. "Just wait there."

DING DONG!

Bertie rubbed his hands. Goodie — more customers! He clattered downstairs. At the door was Angela Nicely and her friend Laura, dressed as witches.

"Trick or treat!" they trilled.

"I'll show you a treat," said Bertie. "How would you like to see a haunted house?"

"Haunted?" cried Angela, wide-eyed. "Is it scary?"

"Very scary," nodded Bertie. "But wait, you're probably too young."

"I'm not! I can tie my own shoelaces," boasted Angela.

"Hmm," said Bertie. "Okay, but it's ten sweets each."

Angela and Laura looked at each other. That was a lot of sweets.

"Let's!" breathed Angela.

Laura shook her head.

"The tour's about to start," said Bertie.

That did it. Angela stepped inside. Bertie helped himself from their bags. This was easy! At this rate, they'd have enough sweets to last them a week.

CHAPTER 4

Nick, Angela and Laura waited outside
Bertie's bedroom door. They had all
been instructed to keep their eyes shut.

"Will it be dark?" trembled Laura.

"VERY dark," said Bertie. "Haunted
houses don't have lights."

"How do you know it's haunted?"
asked Angela.

"I've heard things," said Bertie. "Moaning and groaning."

"And footsteps," added Eugene.

"Huh!" said Nick. "I thought you said you'd actually seen a ghost."

"I have," said Bertie. "A horrible ghost with no eyes."

Laura squeaked.

"Will we see it?" asked Angela.

"Maybe," said Bertie. "Ghosts only come out if you keep really quiet and don't go poking them or anything. Ready?"

He placed his hand on the door handle.

Nick made sure he stayed at the back, just in case. The door creaked open and they crept inside.

"Open your eyes," Bertie whispered in their ears.

They gasped. The room was almost
black, lit only by Mum's scented candles
over by the wall. Something lay on the
bed, covered by a sheet.

"Behold the haunted house of the
mummy," said Bertie dramatically.

"I thought you said it was a ghost,"
said Nick.

"Mummies *are* ghosts," said Bertie. "Anyone knows that."

Laura grasped Angela's hand. "I don't like it," she said. "Let's go."

But Nick wasn't satisfied yet.

"How do we know it's a mummy?" he said. "We can't even see it."

Bertie put a finger to his lips. "We must speak to it," he said. "Say the magic spell after me … O-Y-M-I-Adumbo."

"O-Y-M-I-Adumbo!" They chanted it three times then waited in silence. For a few seconds nothing happened. Then suddenly the sheet twitched. Slowly, stiffly, the figure on the bed sat up. The sheet fell off and a mummified head turned towards them. Laura whimpered. Angela gulped. Nick backed towards the door.

The ghastly mummy moaned.
"URRGHHHH! WHO DARES TO
WAKE ME?" it croaked, starting to rise
from the bed.

"ARGHHH!" screeched the terrified
girls, spilling their sweets.

Dirty Bertie

"LET ME OUT!" wailed Nick, dropping his bag and bolting for the door. They fled from the room, crashing down the stairs three at a time. Nick looked back at the last minute and saw the ancient mummy coming after them.

WHAM! The front door slammed…
Bertie and Eugene burst out laughing.
"HA HA! Did you see Nick's face?"
"And Angela," gasped Eugene.
"I thought she was going to wet herself."
Bertie bent down. "And look what
they left us – all their sweets."
They gathered up the loot.
"Wait a minute," said Eugene, looking
round. "Where's Darren?"

Downstairs in the lounge, Gran was
glued to the TV. A scary vampire film
was reaching the final scene. The
vampire hunter crept down the steps
into Count Dracula's tomb. In the corner
lay a stone coffin. Gran leaned forward.
Behind her the lounge door opened.

"Oh, Bertie," she said. "Come and watch, it's just getting to the good bit!"

She reached for another crisp. Her hand touched something in the bowl. Strangely it didn't feel like Bertie's hand. It was papery and thin, like the hand of a...

"ARGGHHHHHHHHH!"

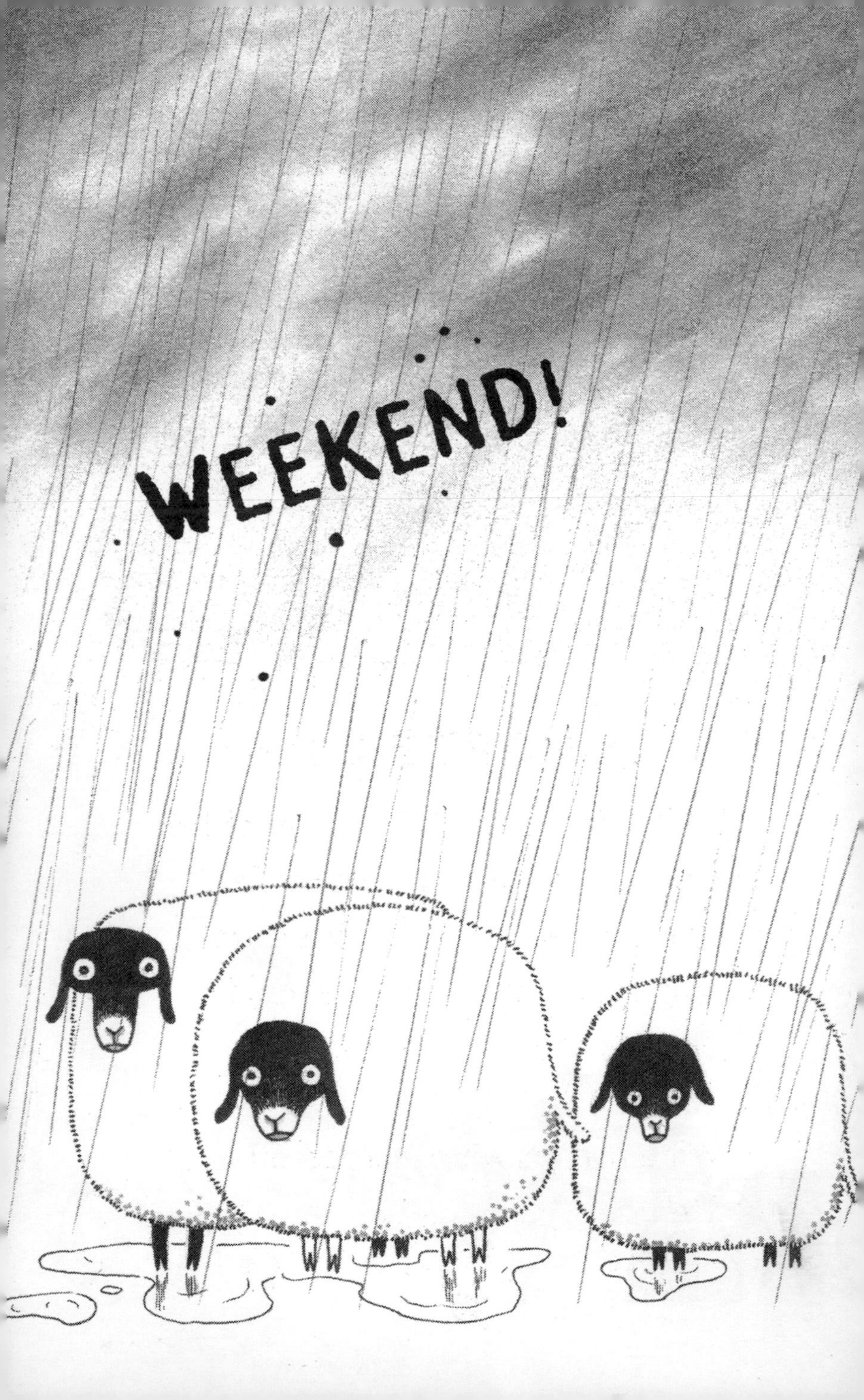
WEEKEND!

CHAPTER 1

SLAM! Bertie was back from school. He flopped on the sofa. *Ahh, Fridays!* he thought, turning on the TV. *Was there anything better?* The whole weekend stretched ahead...

FLOOP!

Wait a minute, who'd turned off the TV?

"Come on," said Mum. "We're going away, remember? You need to pack."

"Going away where?" said Bertie.

"I told you, we're spending the weekend in the country."

Bertie let out a groan. A weekend in the country? What for? Didn't his parents know what the country was like?

"But I want to stay here!" he moaned.

"Don't be silly," said Dad, coming in. "You'll enjoy it."

"Fresh air, sunshine, long walks! It'll be great," said Mum.

Bertie pulled a face. He knew what "long walks" meant – tramping up and down hills in the pouring rain. He had been to the country before and there was nothing to do. No theme parks or pizza parlours, only miles of hills, mud

Dirty Bertie

and cow fields. And you couldn't even step in a cowpat without someone telling you off.

"Why do I have to come?" he grumbled.

"It'll be fun!" said Mum. "We've booked a lovely country cottage." She handed him a leaflet.

Bertie stared at the picture. The cottage was in the middle of nowhere.

"Has it got a swimming pool?" he asked.

"No," said Dad.

"Has it got its own cinema?"

"I doubt it," laughed Mum. "It doesn't even have TV."

NO TV? Were they raving mad? How was he meant to survive a whole weekend without TV? His brain would turn to mush. He might actually DIE of boredom.

"Just think," said Mum. "Two whole days of peace and quiet!"

"I'm taking my books to read," said Suzy, coming into the lounge.

"And I'm taking my binoculars," said Dad. "We can go birdwatching."

Bertie rolled his eyes. Birdwatching? He'd rather do one of Gran's 1000-piece jigsaw puzzles.

Dad glanced at his watch, impatiently.
"If we're going to beat the traffic, we'd
better get going."

"Yes, hurry up and get packed, Bertie,"
said Mum. "There's not much room in
the bags, so only bring what you need."

Bertie stomped upstairs. He threw
open his wardrobe and tossed some
clothes into a heap. What had Mum

41

said — only bring what you need. Well, he would need plenty for a weekend in the country — his comic collection for a start, plus his Dinosaur Hunter's kit. He couldn't leave his Monster Sticker Album behind or his Gunk the Skunk game.

He staggered out of his room as Mum came upstairs to see what was taking so long. She stared. "What's all this?"

"My stuff for the weekend," said Bertie.

"I meant clothes," said Mum. "We haven't got room for all this!"

"But I'll have nothing to do!" moaned Bertie.

"Put them back!" said Mum. "We're only taking essentials."

She hurried back downstairs. Bertie sighed. It wasn't fair. Suzy was taking her books and Katty Kitten Pencil Set. Why couldn't he take what he wanted? He looked at the two bulging bags. One was full of clothes, the other was stuffed with walking gear, including boots, hats and waterproofs. Bertie frowned. "Essentials" Mum had said. But were walking boots essential? Or waterproofs? Bertie could certainly live without them. He emptied out the bag, hiding the boots and coats in Dad's wardrobe. Now he had room for real essentials — like his comic collection and games. Tomorrow, when they were all enjoying a brilliant game of Gunk the Skunk, his family would thank him.

"BERTIE!" Mum called. "Are you packed? We need to go!"

Bertie zipped up the bag quickly. "Coming!" he yelled.

CHAPTER 2

Bertie piled on to the back seat and slammed the car door.

"At last," said Dad, drumming his fingers on the steering wheel.

He started the engine and they set off down the road.

Bertie looked around, puzzled. "Where's Whiffer? Isn't he coming?"

Dirty Bertie

SCREEEEEEECH!

The car skidded to a halt. Dad looked at Mum.

"I thought you put him in," he said.

"No, I left it to YOU," huffed Mum. "I packed everything else."

They drove back to the house. Whiffer was still dozing on his cushion in the kitchen. Bertie hauled him out to the car and heaved him on to the back seat. Once they were all in, it was a bit of a squash.

"Bertie's taking up all the room!" moaned Suzy, as they drove off.

"I am not!" cried Bertie.

"BERTIE!" sighed Mum. "Don't annoy Suzy. Move over."

"It's Whiffer," said Bertie. "He's lolling all over me!"

Mum turned round. "Please don't squabble. We've got a long journey ahead of us."

"How much further?" asked Bertie.

"We're still on our road!" said Dad. "And stop kicking my seat, Bertie!"

Bertie shuffled around, trying to get comfortable. He hated long car journeys. Why did the country have to be miles away? And why didn't his parents get a bigger car? One of those massive stretch limos with room for all his friends.

He stuck his head between the front seats. "I'm hungry!"

"Well, you'll have to wait," said Mum. "We'll eat when we get there."

"But that'll be ages!" protested Bertie.

Mum sighed heavily. "There are snacks in the food bag, but don't stuff yourself or you'll make yourself sick."

Bertie found the bag under Mum's seat. He rummaged around until he found the crisps. Yummy! There were chocolate biscuits, too. No one else seemed to want any, which meant all the more for him.

They joined the motorway and found themselves at the back of a mile-long traffic jam.

Mum closed her eyes. "I don't *believe* it!"

Dad gripped the steering wheel. "I told you we should have left earlier."

Dirty Bertie

"Well, next time maybe YOU should do the packing," snapped Mum.

"I packed *my* stuff!" said Bertie. No one congratulated him. He crammed more crisps into his mouth. "Why have we stopped?"

"IT'S A TRAFFIC JAM!" yelled Mum and Dad at once.

"I only asked!" said Bertie. Honestly, some people were so touchy!

Mum took a deep breath and reached into the glovebox. "Why don't we all listen to a nice quiet story tape?" she suggested.

"YESSSS!" whooped Bertie. "*Monster Wars!*"

"You chose last time!" wailed Suzy. "*Pony Club!*"

"Monsters!"

"Ponies!"

"MON-STERS! MON-STERS! MON-STERS!" chanted Bertie, spitting crisps everywhere.

"QUIET!" yelled Mum. "If you can't agree, we won't listen to either."

They sat in grim silence for a while. Mum turned on the radio and tuned it to some plinky piano music. At last the traffic started to move again. Bertie read

one of his comics while Whiffer dozed in
his lap. Reading sometimes made Bertie
travel sick, but only when he'd eaten too
much. Luckily, he'd only had three bags of
crisps and a packet of chocolate biscuits.

URGLE-URGLE-URGLE!

Bertie's stomach rumbled.

BUUURP!

Come to think of it, he wasn't feeling
so great.

"Mum!" cried Suzy. "Bertie's gone green!"

"WHAT?" gasped Mum, turning round.

"He's going to be sick!" moaned Suzy.

Bertie took deep breaths. He clapped a hand over his mouth. His stomach was heaving like boiling soup.

"STOP THE CAR!" cried Mum.

"Where?" said Dad. "Open the window, Bertie! Take deep breaths!"

Bertie stuck his head out of the window. He took big gulps of air. That helped a little. He sat back down with his head in his hands.

"Try and hang on," said Dad. "Just a few more minutes… We're almost at the—"

BLEUUUUUCH!

Bertie was sick.

Luckily, most of it went on the floor rather than over him.

"EWWW!" cried Suzy, covering her face. "IT STINKS!"

Dad pulled off the motorway and into the service station.

CHAPTER 3

It was dark. It was late. Bertie felt they'd been in the car for weeks. He was feeling better now, though the car still smelt of sick. Mum had taken over the driving while Dad puzzled over the map. Bertie stared gloomily out of the window at the passing fields.

"How far is it now?" he sighed wearily.

"Not far," said Mum. "If your father hasn't got us hopelessly lost."

"I know exactly where we are," said Dad. "We're on this wiggly road that leads to the village."

They drove on for miles before coming to a dead end. The car halted. Mum slumped forward with her head on the steering wheel.

"Ahh," said Dad. "Don't worry, I think I know where we went wrong."

At nine o'clock they turned down a bumpy track and finally came to a stop. Everyone staggered out of the car.

"Honeysuckle Cottage!" said Mum. "Thank heavens!"

An owl hooted. The house was in

Dirty Bertie

total darkness. It looked like the house in a horror film, the one where the family gets murdered.

They found the key under a stone and
went inside. The cottage had heavy
brown curtains, bare floorboards and a
few moth-eaten armchairs.

"Isn't it nice?" said Mum brightly.

"Cosy," agreed Dad.

Bertie held his nose. "POOH! It
smells!"

"Old houses always smell like this,"
said Dad.

Bertie flopped into a chair. So this was
it. They had driven all this way to stay in
a smelly old house with no TV.

Suzy hugged herself. "It's freezing!" she
grumbled.

"Don't worry, it'll soon warm up once
the heating's on," said Mum.

She looked in the kitchen. There was
an ancient boiler in a closet with no sign

of instructions. She pressed a switch and a red light came on.

WHIRR! BONK! CLUNK! It went off again.

"Oh!" said Mum. "I don't think it's working."

"Never mind," said Dad. "I'll get a fire going. We'll have it warm in no time."

Half an hour later they were all huddled on the sofa, wrapped in blankets. A pile of logs smoked damply in the fireplace. Outside, the wind moaned.

"I'm still cold!" complained Suzy.

"I'm shattered," muttered Mum.

"When's supper?" asked Bertie. "You said we'd eat when we got here!"

Dad pulled back the curtains and peered out. "There must be a pub in the village," he said hopefully.

Mum gave him a withering look. "If you think I'm getting in the car again, you've got another think coming," she said.

Dad sighed. "Maybe we should go to bed. We'll all feel better after a good night's sleep."

CHAPTER 4

DONG – DONG – DONG!

The church clock chimed midnight. Lying on the top bunk, Bertie couldn't sleep. No one had warned him the country was such a scary place. Things shrieked and screeched and howled in the night. Worse still, it was so DARK. Their bedroom was blacker than a cave.

Maybe he should go and turn on the landing light? But that meant going OUT THERE where things might be lurking.

CREAK, CREAK!

Bertie sat up. Was that someone coming up the stairs? Maybe it was the bogeyman or a werewolf … or even a bogey-wolf! He poked his head over the side of the bunk beds.

"Suzy? Are you awake?" he hissed.

"Mmm?"

"I can't sleep," moaned Bertie. "I keep hearing noises."

"What sort of noises?" mumbled Suzy.

"Creepy noises – like a werewolf."

"There aren't any werewolves," said Suzy. "They only live in the woods."

Bertie turned pale. There were woods over the road…

Dirty Bertie

Next door, Mum and Dad weren't getting much sleep either. The bedsprings twanged every time one of them rolled over. The mattress was lumpier than a Christmas pudding.

"BAAA! BAAA!"

Dad groaned.

"It's just the sheep," sighed Mum. "It's the country, remember?"

"Don't they ever go to sleep?" grumbled Dad.

"BAAA!"

"Not these sheep," said Mum.

Dad hid his head under the pillow. This was the worst night's sleep he'd ever had. He'd have got more peace and quiet on a motorway.

Feet pattered on the landing. The door creaked open. Dad opened one eye. Bertie stood there in his pyjamas.

"I can't sleep!" he moaned.

"You're not the only one," muttered Dad. "Go back to bed."

"Suzy says the werewolves will eat me," said Bertie.

Mum groaned. "She's making it up."

Dirty Bertie

"Can't I sleep with you?" begged Bertie.

"There isn't room!" said Dad.

"Just for a little bit?" pleaded Bertie. "Please!"

Mum sighed heavily. "All right! But no wriggling."

Twang! Bertie jumped on to the bed and snuggled down between his mum and dad.

"G'night," mumbled Mum.

"Night!" said Bertie.

They all closed their eyes. Five minutes later the door creaked open.

"I can't sleep by myself!" wailed Suzy. "Can I come in with you?"

Morning light spilled through the curtains. Dad squinted at the clock. They had slept in past ten. He shuffled to the window and peeped out. Outside, the rain fell in sheets, making puddles in the yard. Still, they hadn't come all this way to skulk indoors. They'd come for fresh country air. He pulled back the curtains.

"Everybody up! We're going for a walk!"

Suzy rubbed her eyes sleepily. "Do we have to?"

"It's raining!" groaned Bertie.

"A spot of rain won't hurt us," said Dad.

"Dad's right," said Mum. "Besides, we've come prepared. I packed our boots and waterproofs. Where did I leave that bag?"

Uh oh. Bertie slid down under the covers as Mum pulled out the bag and unzipped it. She stared.

"Where are the walking boots?" she gasped. "And all our waterproofs?"

She emptied the bag on to the floor. Out tumbled a jumble of comics, toys and games. Mum sucked in her breath.

"BERTIE!" she yelled.

Bertie's head peeped out.

"Um … anyone want to play Gunk the Skunk?"

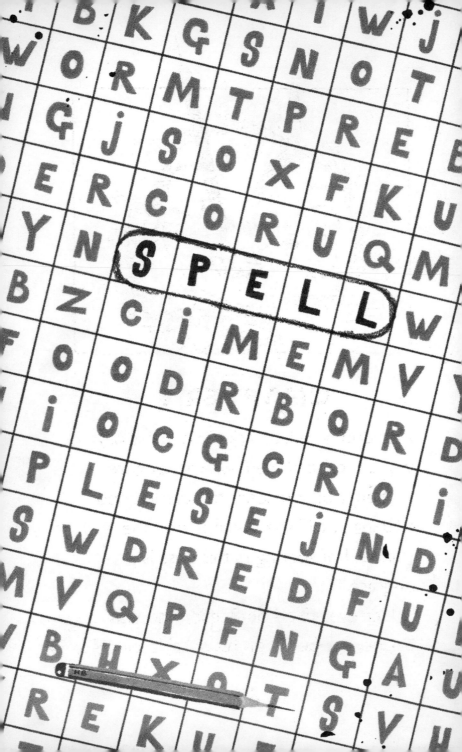

CHAPTER 1

Miss Boot handed back Class 3's history work. She faced them with an icy glare.

"Some of you seem to have learned nothing at all," she barked. "And the standard of spelling in this class is a disgrace."

Her eyes fixed on Bertie, who was balancing a pencil on his nose. It fell off.

"Luckily, there is a chance for a few of you to shine," said Miss Boot. "In two weeks' time it is The Inter-Schools Junior Spelling Bee. Who can tell me what a Spelling Bee is?"

Darren's hand went up. "A bee that's dead clever," he said.

"No, Darren," snapped Miss Boot. "It is a competition. A competition to find the Junior Spelling Bee Champion. Who would like to be a champion?"

Almost every hand shot into the air. Bertie pulled a face. Why did schools always give out prizes for things he couldn't do? What about prizes for annoying teachers or burping the alphabet?

"So, I will be choosing two lucky children who…"

Miss Boot droned on and on. Bertie stopped listening. He looked up at the cracks in the ceiling, wondering how soon it would fall down.

"…so as a special treat, we are going to have a spelling test!" said Miss Boot.

Bertie sat up in wild panic. Not a *spelling test*! Last time he'd come bottom of the class. Miss Boot had sent a note home to his parents, who'd threatened to stop his pocket money if he didn't improve. He had to think of a way to get a good mark.

Ten minutes later he stared gloomily at his answer sheet:

He'd guessed most of the answers, though maybe one or two were wrong. Did "Stupid" have one "o" or two? He glanced around the class. Eugene was checking his work. Darren was doodling. Know-All Nick sat back wearing a smug grin. *Trust smarty-pants to know all the answers*, thought Bertie. Wait a minute…

Dirty Bertie

He'd just had a brilliant idea.

"Right," barked Miss Boot. "Write your names on your papers and pass them forward."

"Hey, Nick!" hissed Bertie. "Isn't that your mitten?"

"Where?" Nick turned pink. His mum always made him wear mittens to school.

"Under your chair," said Bertie.

Nick ducked down to look.

SHWOOP!

Bertie swiped Nick's answer sheet.

Quick as a flash, Bertie wrote his name on it and scrawled "NICHOLAS" on his own. There, that should do it. He passed both papers forward, just in time.

"There's nothing— Hey, where's my spelling test?" squawked Nick.

"It's okay, I handed it in," smiled Bertie.

"But I didn't write my name on it!"

"Don't worry, I did it for you," said Bertie.

Nick frowned. Bertie wasn't normally so helpful. What was he up to?

ORFUL

After break, Class 3 trooped back inside. Miss Boot was waiting for them.

"I have marked your spelling tests and I am not impressed," she said. "Some of you can't even spell your own name.

However, I'm pleased to say that two of you got very high marks."

Know-All Nick beamed. He was bound to come top.

"Donna, you scored 17 out of 20 – excellent," said Miss Boot. "But one of the class scored full marks and that was…" She swallowed hard. "That was … er, Bertie."

Everyone gasped and turned their heads.

"BERTIE?" howled Nick, in disgust.

"Thank you, Nicholas," said Miss Boot.

"But Miss, I got them all—"

"THAT WILL DO, NICHOLAS!" thundered Miss Boot. "As it happens, you came bottom of the class. You could learn a lot from Bertie's hard work."

Bertie turned and stuck out his tongue.

Miss Boot went on. "So we have two clear winners: Donna and Bertie. They will be entering the Junior Spelling Bee next week."

Bertie almost choked. *What?* Him – in the Spelling Bee? Miss Boot had to be kidding! When was this decided?

"But Miss…" he spluttered. "I can't!"

"Nonsense!" snapped Miss Boot.

"Spelling's bad for me. I come out in a rash," said Bertie.

Dirty Bertie

"Don't be ridiculous," barked Miss Boot. "You came top of the class, so I shall be expecting great things from you. Is that clear, Bertie?"

Bertie nodded miserably. He'd been in some tight spots before, but how on earth was he going to get out of this one?

CHAPTER 2

That evening, over supper, Bertie broke the terrible news to his parents.

"A Spelling Bee?" frowned Dad. "But don't you need to be good at spelling?"

"Yes!" moaned Bertie.

"So how come they picked you?" grinned Suzy.

"I don't know, it was a mistake!"

said Bertie.

He could hardly explain that he'd cheated in a spelling test.

"Well, your spelling must have improved a lot," said Mum. "That's brilliant, Bertie."

"But I can't do the Spelling Bee!" wailed Bertie. "It'll be a disaster!"

"Of course it won't," said Mum. "Just do your best."

"You don't understand, I'm rubbish at spelling!"

"Well, Miss Boot doesn't think so," said Dad. "Anyway, you just have to learn the words."

"I can't learn all of them!" cried Bertie. "There are millions!"

"We'll help you," said Mum. "We'll make a list of twenty spellings every night for you to learn."

Bertie gaped. Twenty spellings every night? That would take him forever! He would have to give up watching TV and eating meals! In any case, he didn't need *more* spelling, he got enough of it at school! It was all Know-All Nick's fault. If he wasn't such a clever clogs, none of this would have happened!

STOOPID

The day of the Spelling Bee arrived. Bertie found himself with all the other contestants in a room off St Mildred's school hall. Already the hall was filling up with excited school parties. Bertie wished he was sitting in the audience with his friends. His opponents all looked like nerds and brainiacs. They probably went over spellings in their sleep.

"You okay, Bertie?" asked Donna, coming over. "You don't look well."

"I'm fine," replied Bertie. "It's only a spelling contest. I mean, who cares?"

"Miss Boot," said Donna. "Still, as long as we don't go out in the first round."

"How do you mean?" said Bertie.

Donna looked at him. "Don't you know? If you get one word wrong, you're out."

Dirty Bertie

"OUT?" said Bertie. "No clues, no second chances?"

Donna shook her head. "That's the rules. One mistake and you're dead."

Bertie gulped. Spelling bees were brutal! What if he went out in the first round? Miss Boot would blow a fuse. He'd be doing spelling tests for the rest of his life!

Someone tapped him on the shoulder.

"It's only me," said Eugene. "Just came to wish you luck."

Bertie pulled him to one side. "Eugene, you've got to get me out of this!" he begged. "I can't go out there, I'll look like an idiot."

"You *are* an idiot," grinned Eugene.

Bertie dragged him to the boys' toilets and closed the door behind them.

Dirty Bertie

"Listen, I've got to tell you something," he said. "I cheated in the spelling test. I swapped papers with Know-All Nick."

"YOU DIDN'T!" gasped Eugene. "Does Miss Boot know?"

"Of course she doesn't, that's why she picked me for this!" moaned Bertie.

"Well, what are you going to do?" asked Eugene.

"You're good at spelling," said Bertie desperately. "You'll have to help me."

"ME?" cried Eugene. "I can't! I'll be in the audience."

"Exactly," said Bertie. "So no one will know. You don't even have to speak, just give me a clue."

"Like what?" asked Eugene.

Bertie scratched his head. "You know, if the letter's 'I' then point to your eye."

"But what if the letter's 'P'?" said Eugene.

"I don't know, think of something!" cried Bertie.

Eugene looked worried. "It'll never work. Miss Boot will be watching. What if we get caught?"

"We won't," said Bertie. "Please, Eugene, you're my only hope!"

CHAPTER 3

The contestants sat on the stage with numbers pinned to their chests. Bertie was wearing number thirteen. He stared out at the audience nervously. Miss Boot was in the third row. Know-All Nick sat along from her, pulling faces at him. Bertie spotted Eugene next to Darren a few rows back.

Dirty Bertie

The girl wearing number one made the long walk to the microphone. She stood trembling in the spotlight. The Reader's voice boomed out, giving her a word to spell.

"CLOUDY. It was a cloudy sky. CLOUDY."

The girl let out a faint squeak. She screwed her eyes tight shut.

"C-L…" she began. "Um…" She fell

silent then gabbled the rest. "-O-W-D-Y.
CLOWDY."

There was a deathly silence.

"I'm sorry," boomed the Reader. "That
is not correct. Thanks for taking part."

"Waaa-haa!" The girl fled from the
stage sobbing.

Bertie watched the other children
plod to the front, one by one. Suddenly
Donna nudged him. Yikes! He was next!

He stumbled out to the microphone, tripping on a wire and bumping into it. The audience giggled. Bertie rubbed his head.

"DRIPPING," boomed the Reader. "The tap was dripping. DRIPPING."

Bertie groaned. He was hoping for something easy – like DOG or LOG. He stared at Eugene, who had turned red and sunk down in his seat.

"D!" yelled Bertie, deafening the front row. Eugene gave a small nod.

"D ... um ... R..." said Bertie. Eugene winked an eye. "I!" cried Bertie.

D-R-I ... what next? His mind had gone blank. Eugene rolled his eyes then screwed up his face and started to bounce up and down in his seat.

"BONKERS!" cried Bertie.

"I'm sorry?" said the Reader.

Bertie shook his head. Bonkers wasn't a letter. What on earth was Eugene trying to say? He was jiggling about as if he was in pain or needed the loo. *That's it*, thought Bertie. *Loo, poo, wee, widdle, pee-pee. Yes, PP!*

"D-R-I-P-P..." said Bertie. Almost there, he could do this. "...I-N-G. DRIPPING."

"Correct!"

The audience clapped. Bertie almost fainted with relief. Miss Boot mopped her face. Bertie bowed, clonking the microphone again, then marched back to his place. Spelling wasn't so tough. Actually, he was pretty good at it. With a bit of help from Eugene, he might even win!

CHAPTER 4

After the interval four children came
back on stage for the final round. Donna
had gone out, but to everyone's
amazement Bertie was still there. He
had spelled ten words correctly – even
"Vegetable" – a word he never used.
Now it was him against the other three.
One of them would become Junior

Dirty Bertie

Spelling Bee Champion. Bertie glanced at the silver trophy sitting to one side. He imagined Know-All Nick's face when he showed it off in assembly.

Miss Boot was edging along a row to get to her seat. Wait a minute … she had moved! She was sitting down next to Eugene! Bertie went cold. This was terrible! How was Eugene meant to help him with Miss Boot in the next seat?

The final round began. Giles, Harriet
and Yuko all spelt their words correctly.
Then it was Bertie's turn. He dragged
himself to the microphone. He gazed
out at the rows of faces, feeling dizzy.
Miss Boot was watching him like a hawk.
Please, please, let it be something easy,
he prayed.

Dirty Bertie

"UNUSUAL," boomed the Reader.

Bertie's mouth fell open. "Unusual?"
What kind of word was that? It had
about a million letters! He looked at
Eugene for help. But Eugene shook his
head. Bertie was on his own. *Think —
what's the first letter of "unusual"?*

"UUUOOOAAHH…" he mumbled.

"Pardon?" said the Reader. "Can you
speak up?"

Bertie wiped the
sweat from his
brow. Maybe he
could pretend to
pass out?

"I'll have to hurry
you," said the Reader.

Bertie took a deep breath. There was
nothing for it, he'd have to take a guess.

"U-N…" he began. "Y-O … um … O
… O-J-A-L. UNYOOOJAL."

"I'm sorry, that's not correct,"
said the Reader.

Miss Boot groaned
and buried her head
in her hands. Bertie
sighed. He'd given it
his best shot.
He took a bow,
headbutting the
microphone again.

ScooL

Afterwards, Donna and Bertie joined the
rest of their class in the hall.

"Well done, Donna," said Miss Boot.
"You did ever so well."

"What about me?" said Bertie. "I got

to the final round."

"Yes, indeed," said Miss Boot. "Nicholas pointed out to me that you kept looking at Eugene."

"Did I?" said Bertie, turning pink.

"You did," said Miss Boot, frostily. "Every time you were stuck."

"Um, well…" mumbled Bertie.

"That's why I moved seats at the interval," Miss Boot went on. "Then, strangely, your spelling went to pieces. I wonder why that was?"

"Um … bad luck, I s'pose," muttered Bertie.

Miss Boot narrowed her eyes. "Hmm. If I find out that you were cheating, Bertie, you will find yourself in *very* hot water."

She turned and stormed off.

Bertie gulped. He just hoped his secret was safe with Eugene – otherwise it spelt T-R-O-U-B-L-E!